The Story of
The Faded Fobs

This story shows the values of helping out
when a friend is in need and of liking
who and what we are.

Story by:
Ken Forsse

Illustrated by:
David High
Russell Hicks
Valerie Edwards
Rennie Rau

WORLDS OF WONDER™

Grubby™ Newton Gimmick™ Princess Aruzia™ Leota™ Wooly What's-It™ Prince Arin™ Fobs™

One day Grubby and I were in Boggley Woods picking wild strawberries.

Page 1

Strawberry picking takes a lot of energy.

Two hands are better than one.

It was the sound of lots
of little furry Fobs.

Look at us, we're grey!

Hey, that stuff is sticky.

The Fobs were right,
not a drop of water
anywhere. Rainbow
Falls had dried up.

We watched Wooly as he climbed up the side of the mountain.

All the Fobs began drinking the colored water.

There was a big rock
blocking the waterfall.

I am proud to be me.